Breaking
THE Promise

KAY WILLIAMS

ISBN 978-1-63630-250-8 (Paperback)
ISBN 978-1-63630-251-5 (Hardcover)
ISBN 978-1-63630-252-2 (Digital)

Covenant Books, Inc.
11661 Hwy 707
Murrells Inlet, SC 29576
www.covenantbooks.com

To my children:

Sunshine

Pumpkin

Goldenboy

Chapter 1

Sitting on the sofa, Hanna grabbed her sneakers, putting them on to take an early morning jog. She decided to run to the park by her apartment. It was Saturday and to get her started, she needed a run so she would stop procrastinating cleaning her apartment and changing her bedding. She wasn't really domestic, but she loved to cook, but cleaning was another story.

Opening the door, she met Bobby, her next door neighbor's little boy who would take care of Gilly, her goldfish, when she went away. She would go to Boston to visit her parents several times a year. Hanna liked animals but thought it cruel to not be with them all day. Her life was too busy for anything right now she thought, except a goldfish or any tropical fish, but Gilly, her goldfish, worked just fine for her now. He was someone to come home to after a long day at work. She thought he even talk to her sometimes with his bubbles.

"Hi, Bobby, how are you today?"

"I am fine. How is Gilly?" Bobby replied.

"He is doing great, but he misses you. Come see him soon. Bye, Bobby, going for a run in the park."

She hit the street running. It was a beautiful warm day in Philadelphia where she now lived for several years. She headed straight for the park. Loved the weekends; they were her relaxing times to unwind and enjoy her life the way she wanted to. She had no one to answer to but her parents, and they were in Boston and didn't visit her that often. She would go visit them, or a short visit with a friend back home.

She loved to explore the city. Sometimes nothing more than a trip to the donut shop to watch the people or her weekly trip to the library for her weekly reading. Sometimes to the movies with a coworker. She loved her life at this point—free to do as she pleased. Today, she was enjoying her run in the park, noticing all the people jogging and relaxing as she was doing. She ran about four miles around the park and then headed home to clean.

All afternoon, she spent cleaning and getting laundry; caught up ready to go back to work the next week. She worked hard and long hours as a receptionist in a busy doctor's office. She loved her work, and the patients loved her. She had worked there for three years. She was devoted to her work.

On Saturday, she decided she had read all her library books, so off she went for her walk to the library to get her reading for the next week. She liked to read at night before she went to sleep. The news sometimes kept her awake. She decided to watch it early and read at night, more relaxing, grabbing her books and jacket and took off for the library. The library was only five blocks away from the apartment, just a nice stroll. She liked walking in her neighborhood, nice people around her area. Gardens blooming, birds singing, and butterflies were everywhere. Before long, she opened the door to the library, turned in her books, and went to the areas she liked to get her books from—mysteries, history, and maybe a romance. After picking her books, she went to sit down and decide which ones she would take home to read for the week. She read the short summaries and decided on two mysteries, one history, and one romance.

As she read at the table, she looked up to see that everyone at the table had left but one man sitting at the other end. As she looked up, so did he. They looked at each other in amazement; to discover they had a lot of similarities. Her hair was ash brown, his also; he had brown eyes, she had hazel. They were both fair-skinned. Faces were shaped oblong with small noses and close to the same age and close in height. They both noticed the similarity and smiled at each other and went back to what they were doing. Hanna gathered up her books as he gather up his briefcase and closed it. He looked at her and said, "They say everyone has a look-alike. I guess we have found ours." She smiled at him as he left, and she went to check out her books.

Walking back down the street, she smiled as she thought, *Man, he could pass as my long lost brother.* She smiled, knowing she was an only child. She got home to see Bobby by her door wanting to see Gilly. "Come on in, Bobby. You can feed Gilly today. He hasn't eaten yet. Remember, not too much. He is just a little fish."

Bobby agreed. He sat and watched him swim around and around till his mother called and asked Hanna to send Bobby home. They were going away for a while. Hanna told

Bobby that his mother wanted him. She told him to come back soon; Gilly missed him. Bobby told her, "Okay," and left.

Chapter 2

Grant walked in the front door to see Ella getting dinner ready. "What's for dinner?"

Ellie smiled and said, "How does baked ham, mash potatoes, and a nice salad sound?"

Grant smiled and said, "Great. I'll be right back to help after I get rid of my briefcase and change my clothes."

"Take your time. I have it under control," she said.

She loved being a housewife, mother, and girl Friday. Grant and Ella had been married for ten years. They had a son, Michael, who was eight. Their only child; they wanted more but never happened. Michael was a great son; filled their lives with a lot of happiness. The years were flying by so fast as Ella would look at Michael and could hardly believe he was eight years old soon-to-be nine. She dreaded the day he would no longer be their little boy, but he was very close to them now and that pleased her.

Grant was back in the kitchen to help. He leaned over and gave Ella a big hug and kissed her with all the love they shared. She looked at him and said, "I hate it when you have to work on a Saturday," which most of the time, that meant he had to go out of town for the weekend. He smiled and agreed. Both knew it couldn't be helped. Grant was a lawyer for an engineering firm; his hours never seem to be eight—four or five days a week—but the money was good, and he liked the firm and people he worked for and with.

"By the way, I am going to make a trip to Boston next week for the meeting I told you about. I will only be gone on Saturday, catching commuter Saturday morning, back Sunday morning before noon," Grant stated. She didn't like any of the trips he made. She hated sleeping alone. "We will have the rest of Sunday together with Michael," Grant said.

The telephone rang. It was Hanna's mother calling from Boston. "We haven't heard from you in a while, are you okay?"

"Yes, Mom, I am fine."

"Why don't you come see us?" her mother asked. "Spend a long weekend with us? Hanna, we aren't getting any younger you know, and we miss you."

"I know, Mom, I was thinking of coming up next week. I know Dad has a birthday next week, and we can all celebrate it together. What will he be, thirty-nine?"

Her mother laughed. "Maybe just a little bit older than that, but he runs circles around me! So we will see you next weekend?" her mother asked.

"Yes, till next weekend. I love you both. Bye."

Hanna started to think of what she would do to be able to have a long weekend with her parents. She would have to talk to Bobby about feeding Gilly and getting her father a birthday gift. That would take time. Clothing? No. Tools? No. Then she thought a gift card from Lowe's. He liked to garden, maybe there was something he needed that she didn't know. She decided to get him the gift card and a box of his favorite candy, chocolate-covered peanuts. She was satisfied he would like that. Got her laundry caught up and packed her suitcase, and she was good to go.

Hanna had to make her short trip commuter train arrangements yet. She would do that in the middle of the week. Never had problems waiting till then to do it. Plans were made. Now just the waiting to go.

Tuesday night, Hanna called Bobby to see if he would come over after school some evening this week, so she could talk to him about feeding Gilly when she left for the weekend, hoping he was going to be home to do this for her while she went to Boston to see her parents.

Sometimes, she felt as if the preparations for the short trip took longer than the time she spent with her parents, but she always felt it was worth it when she got there.

Chapter 3

Grant was getting ready for his trip. Lots of phone calls to make to set up meetings when he got there. Work to get done in the office so he would feel free to go and know things would run smooth for the overnight trip when he was gone.

Ted knocked on Grant's office door, his best friend and coworker. "Hey, buddy, what can I do to help you get ready to go?"

Grant said, "I am already to go. Commuter leaves at 8:00 a.m. tomorrow morning so I am good to go."

Ted stated, "If you forget something, just call and I will take care of it."

Grant smiled and said, "I know you always have my back."

It was getting close to quitting time, so Ted wished Grant good luck on his trip. Grant said he would call him if he needed something, but stated he was pretty sure he would do fine. Ted told him he would see him Monday morning and closed the door and was gone. Grant got his briefcase and put all his work in it. He looked around the office to see nothing was missed to do, closed the door, and headed home to spend the night with Ella and Mike. Knowing they hated his trips, even though they were short and on the weekends. Maybe that was why they both hated it. They liked him home with them on the weekends.

Mike had friends to do things with now since he was getting older, such as playing ball and riding bikes to the park. Ella had friends, but their husbands were home with them, so she wasn't happy with Grant's trips. The company he dealt with in Boston always liked to do their out-of-town meetings on Saturdays. Grant could not understand why, but he wanted their business, and he didn't have to do it a lot so he agreed to the meetings.

At seven thirty, Hanna was up and on her way to the station to catch the commuter. Grant was hugging Mike in bed and getting his suitcase and briefcase and heading downstairs for his kiss from Ella. She had a cup of coffee ready, and Grant kissed her and drank the coffee. He told her he would get breakfast on the train; it would give him something to do on the trip to Boston. It took three and a half hours to get there.

Commuter was ready to go at eight o'clock sharp with everyone on board. Everyone was settling in; some had magazines and books to read to kill the travel time. Others were talking to each other whom they came with. After it started to move, some people were moving around to go to a small dining room in the middle of the two large cars.

As Hanna sat reading a book, she saw Grant go by her seat. He was headed for the dining car to get breakfast. She looked in shock at him and remembered he was the gentleman in the library whom she thought favored her in his looks. She went back to reading her book, but the thought was still in her mind. Thirty minutes, he went back to his seat, and she was sure it was him. The commuter train stopped in Boston, and they all got off, but she didn't see him depart. Hanna gathered up all her things and got off also. When she departed, there was her father looking for her. She ran to him, gave him a big hug, and asked about her mother. Her father explained her mother was home fixing a special lunch for her—all her favorites!

Chapter 4

They got to the house up the front walk; remember as a little girl how she loved the house she lived in and still did when she came home for visits. Her mother greeted her as she opened the door. The smells of all her favorite food. They sat down to a lovely lunch. Hanna loved her mother's cooking and missed it. They sat in the living room and caught up on all the town gossip and everything new in Hanna's life, which wasn't much; seemed to be same old, same old. It seemed just right for Hanna, but her mother wanted more for her, like someone nice in her life to share it with her. Hanna kept telling her she was fine as is, but Mom kept trying to talk her into a mate. The next day was her father's birthday, and they had a few neighbors over to have a little party, and Hanna gave her father his gift, which he loved. Said this week he would use his gift card and buy some supplies he needed to plant his garden this year, and he passed around the candy she had gotten him. It was a nice day for Hanna, and she knew it would be hard to leave them in the morning to catch the commuter back to Philadelphia. The next morning, they had a lovely breakfast, and Hanna hugged her parents and promised to come back soon for a longer visit. They would miss her. She was their only child whom they loved deeply.

She got to the commuter and was settling down with her book and noticed Grant wasn't on the commuter. Hanna had taken the morning off and was going in at noon to work.

When she got to her apartment, Bobby was coming out and said, "I just fed Gilly." She thanked him for taking good care of her goldfish and gave him ten dollars for doing such a good job. He ran into his apartment across the hall loudly telling his mother he just earned a lot of money from Hanna for the great job he did. Hanna smiled to herself and put her luggage down and got herself a cup of coffee from her one-cup coffee maker. She was home to start another week at work.

The next week was a busy time in the doctor's office. On Wednesday after work, Hanna got home and decided to take a run before she ate her dinner. Putting on her jogging outfit and sneakers and out the door she went.

She ran to the park and decided to sit on the park bench to enjoy the people and the surrounding at the park and relax a bit. As she sat down, she noticed another lady sitting at the end of her bench, just enjoying the park also. She began to talk to her. Ella introduced herself to Hanna, and she said how much she enjoyed the park. She told Hanna her husband and son would soon be home for dinner, but she was taking a little break because they would be late tonight. Her son was playing baseball tonight, and her husband would pick him up on his way home from work, and they would have a late dinner together. Hanna told Ella how much she liked coming to the park and running several times a week there. Ella said she just liked to walk there and sit and enjoy nature. It was so pretty in the spring and fall and finally she said, "Really, I enjoy it all the time," and laughed. The people are so friendly. They talked for a while and then Ella said that she should head home to put the finishing touches on dinner and that her family would soon be there, and Hanna agreed she should finish her run. They both got up, but as they were saying goodbye, Ella dropped to the sidewalk, and Hanna bent down to see if she was okay. There was no response when Hanna said, "Ella, Ella." Hanna checked for her breathing and a heartbeat and couldn't feel anything. People were starting to gather around, and Hanna called 911. They were asking what happened, and Hanna told them. By then, the ambulance was coming down the street. They asked Hanna a few questions, and Hanna told them very little about Ella and that they had just met. They did some vitals and then put her in the ambulance and was gone. Hanna went back to her apartment in a daze. She felt so helpless not knowing anymore about the lady she was talking to.

Chapter 5

She looked in the paper the next day but found nothing about it. She looked every day for two weeks and found nothing. One Saturday, she was going through her old papers before throwing them out, and in one of the old papers, she saw in the obituaries where a lady died after suffering from a heart attack. Just things about her life and her family made her read more. It stated that her husband was a legal lawyer for an engineering firm, about a young son and his name. Hanna had a strong feeling when she read the article that this was the lady in the park whom she helped. It gave an address, which was only five blocks from her apartment. She decided on Sunday that she would walk up the street to the block she read in the paper where this house was. She took a walk and looked at the house; it was a real nice house. Hanna saw a young boy sitting on the front porch. She turned and walked back to her apartment wondering if that was her son. Now she knew their names. Ella was the lady who died. Her husband name was Grant Wilson, and his son's name was Michael.

Hanna went to work the next day. On Tuesday evening, she decided to walk up the street to Ella's house again. It was a nice cool evening; the sun was setting, and it was calm as she approached the house. She saw a man bent over planting flowers in the flowerbed out front of the porch. She wanted to ask him about his wife and tell him how she knew her. As she walked up the sidewalk, he got up and looked at her as she approached. Her mouth opened in astonishment as he stood up. It was the man in the library and on the commuter. He looked at her in amazement, and she stared at him. Both smiled. She introduced herself, and he told her his name, and she said she knew. She began to tell him she was the one who called 911 in the park when his wife became ill and fainted. He stated that his wife had a heart attack and was in a coma for a week and then passed away. Tears flowed down his cheeks as he stood there, and Hanna asked about his son. He said he was going to counseling and holding his own. She hugged him and said how sorry she was. She asked if she could come back now and then to talk to him.

He hugged her and said anytime. He enjoyed company at this time. When she hugged him, it felt strange—like she knew him. He told her, "Thank you for being there with his wife at that time." She walked away and said she would come back for another visit.

She got back to her apartment and tried to watch some television to take her mind off Ella's family. It didn't work for her, so she decided to read, got her bath, and went to bed with a book to read, and then decided to go to sleep. About 2:00 a.m., she finally fell asleep. The next day, she went to work, but often thought of Grant and Mike. She had several days thinking of them. She decided to make them dinner and take it to them. She made a meatloaf and baked some potatoes and fruit salad, put them in the car, and drove to their house. She got out with the box and knocked on the door. Mike answered the door and then called to his father and said a lady was at the door. Grant came, smiled, and said, "Please come in."

Hanna said she brought them a hot dinner and told them what it was. He said they would take it if she would stay and eat with them. Hanna smiled and said, "Okay, I make a mean meatloaf."

They both smiled, and Grant led her to the kitchen. It was a beautiful home. They sat down and ate. Grant said she was an angel because he was sweating over what they were going to eat. They all enjoyed the meal. Mike was very quiet, but he started to talk after dinner a little. Hanna asked him about baseball, and he was interested in her interest in baseball. When she went to leave, they both asked her to come back and if she wanted to, she could try another meal on them. They all laughed and said goodbye. Hanna felt better this time when she left.

She got in the car and drove to her apartment, thinking how sorry she was about Ella's death. If ever a family deserved to be together, she thought it was theirs.

When she walked in her apartment, the phone rang, and it was Grant thanking her again and asked if she would go to dinner with them. "Mike enjoyed your company, and it did him good," Grant said. "So please let us take you to dinner."

Hanna said, "I would be delighted to go, just call with a time and the date."

Grant said it would be next week sometime and he would call. He thanked her again for such a nice evening. It sure was a nice change.

She hung up the phone and then picked up a book to sit down and read when the phone rang again. Hanna thought, *Boy, what a busy day*. It was her mother asking how she was doing. Hanna told her she was doing fine. Her mother told Hanna how her father enjoyed his birthday and her gifts she gave him. "He ate all the rest of the candy you got him," she said. Hanna laughed and asked if she got any. Her mother stated, "Not one piece!" Hanna chuckled. They talked a little longer and then agreed it was time for bed. Hanna promised to call again soon and hung up, telling her mother that she loved them very much. She went to bed with her book but was too tired to even open it. She went right to sleep.

The next day was busy at the office and when Bobby came over and fed Gilly, he talked to Hanna for a while and then went home. She couldn't get Michael and Grant off her mind. The phone rang. It was Grant. "How does Tuesday night sound, a dinner and movie?"

Hanna said, "It sounds great."

They talked a little while about how beautiful the weather has been and then hung up. Hanna was anxious to see them again.

Chapter 6

Tuesday evening came quickly. She was all ready when they came to pick her up. They went to a great restaurant and saw a good movie—Mike picked it out. It was a great mystery movie right up Hanna's alley. They all had a good time. Grant drove to Hanna's apartment and said, "The evening went much too quickly." She invited them to come up to the apartment, but Grant said, "Mike has school tomorrow. Could they take a rain check?"

Hanna smiled and said, "Sure."

Hanna went straight to bed wanting to finish the book she was reading, but discovered she was too tired and was asleep in no time.

She went to work the next day and when she got home, she decided to take a jog to the park. Hanna went to the bench where she met Ella and sat for a long time. On the way home, she saw Mike walking up the street to his house. She stopped and talked to him for a while, and they talked about the movie they saw. Mike said there was another one he wanted to see and wondered if Hanna would like to come with them to see it. She said, "Sure." He smiled and said he better get home before his father started to worry about him. They said goodbye and went on their different ways. As Hanna jogged home, her heart ached for Mike. He was such a good boy, and she knew he had a great dad to help him with his sorrow.

Two days later, the phone rang when she got home. It was Grant. "Hello, Mike said he asked you to a movie, and I am tossing in dinner. How about Saturday night about six thirty we pick you up?"

Hanna said, "That sounds good."

They went to a nice restaurant and had dinner and then watched a good movie they all liked. They had such a good time together. Mike said, "I am so tired. Could you drop me off?"

Grant said, "Sure. I would just be gone a minute to drop Hanna off at her apartment, and I would be right back."

When they got to her apartment, she leaned over and kissed Grant on the cheek and said what a good time she had and thanked him for the dinner and nice evening.

He drove away, not knowing how to handle the kiss on the cheek. He knew he had to explain to Hanna about still loving Ella, and he would not want a relationship with anyone for a long time yet. All night, Grant worried about how he would talk to Hanna and explain it to her without hurting her feelings or losing her friendship. Both Mike and Grant cherished her friendship and didn't want to jeopardize that. He was so in love with Ella that he knew it would take a long time for him to think about anyone else like he loved his wife. He was hoping Hanna would understand because he liked being with her and would feel bad if it ended their friendship now. He and Mike both looked forward to spending time with her and doing things.

The next day, Grant couldn't get his mind off telling Hanna how he felt, just then a knock at his office door. Grant looked up and saw Ted. "Come on in. You are just the guy I need to talk to," Grant said. "Ted, shut the door and sit down in the chair please."

"What is up, buddy?" Ted asked.

Grant told Ted about the situation with Hanna. Ted looked at Grant, smiled, and said, "Just tell her how you feel. If she truly likes you and Mike, she will understand."

Grant called Hanna that night on the phone and told her how he felt, hoping she would understand and hoped that she would be good enough with a friendship. Hanna smiled into the phone and said, "Okay, no more kisses on the cheek!"

Grant laughed. "Will it be okay if I call you this weekend for dinner and a movie?"

Hanna replied, "Sounds good to me. See you on the weekend. Call with the day and time." As Hanna sat on the sofa thinking of Grant, she smiled and thought, *What a nice guy*. She decided to call her mom and talk to her. "Hi, Mom, how are you?"

She said she was fine and so was Hanna's father busy working in his garden. "How are you, honey?" her mother asked.

"I'm fine," she replied. Hanna told her mom about being friends with Grant and Mike and how she enjoyed doing things with them. She told her mother about how she had met Grant at the library and the tragedy of Ella's death, and how she was in the park with her when she became ill, and she called 911 for her, but she died. She told her how she then met Grant again and it was funny, but they had a resemblance to each other. She told her mother they became friends through this tragedy and were doing things together. Her mother told her how sorry she was for their family and how proud she was of her. She told Hanna how everyone has a double; this might be her double. Betsy (Hanna's mom) said that she needed to go; her father was looking for something and needed her help to find it. So, she hung up, telling Hanna she loved her. "Tell Dad I love him, and I will call again soon. Bye, Mom."

Chapter 7

Grant called Hanna and asked her for dinner and a movie on Saturday at seven. He said, "Mike had plans with a friend, would that be okay?"

Hanna said, "Sure."

They saw a great movie and had a late dinner. It was terrific. Grant felt good they were both relaxed and having a great time. When he took her to her apartment, she asked if he wanted to come up for a cup of coffee. Grant smiled and said, "Yes, Mike was staying over at his friend's house."

They had a nice time talking over three cups of coffee. Hanna told Grant about her family that she was an only child. Grant also was an only child and said he was adopted. She asked if he ever wanted to know his real parents, and he stated no because he loved his father and mother, and he was a baby when he was adopted. They were the only people he knew, and that was good enough for him. Everything he needed a great childhood and was sent to one of the best colleges to become a lawyer. They were both dead now and said he felt bad. They were alive when he married Ella, but both died shortly after that; his father was first and then his mother. He said she missed his father so much. He thought that was why she died so soon after he did. Grant said he and Ella felt badly. They knew they would have loved knowing their first grand-child. Hanna reached across the table and put her hand on his. He looked up, smiled, and said, "No kisses."

She laughed.

Grant got up, hugged Hanna, and said he had a great time.

She said, "Me, too. Take care."

Grant left, thinking how lucky he was to have a friend like Hanna.

Hanna went to bed thinking about the evening and wondering what would come of this relationship. Hanna wanted someone in her life but knew Grant was so in love with Ella that nothing would happen in this rela-tionship for a long time. She decided that he was such a good person that this friendship was good enough at this time in her life. She went to bed and thought of Grant and Mike and if nothing but the friendship was in the future, that would be good enough. They certainly needed just a good friend in their lives right now, and she guessed she was it.

Hanna, Grant, and Mike spent a lot of time together enjoying movies, dinners, picnics, and walks in the park. They would meet there sometimes after work and then go to dinner. Mike was doing good, no longer going for counseling. Grant was so proud of him. They had each other, and that was great in Grant's mind. Mike was such a good help to Grant. He sometimes helped get a quick dinner, as well as helped with cleaning and laundry. He had great friends, too. Grant never worried about him. He had good grades in school, and he felt well blessed with his son. Grant saw a lot of Ella in his son—so giving to help others and so strong when he needed to be. Grant missed Ella terribly but never let on to Mike. They went together several times to put roses on Ella's grave and then left silently, both with their own thoughts of missing her. They were slowly adjusting and thanked Hanna a lot for that. They would each talk to her about missing Ella, and she would help them with their grief and make them realize that life went on and to cherish their memories of Ella.

Chapter 8

Hanna was at her desk in the office doing her scheduling of patients for the next day when the phone rang, and it was her father. Her parents never called her at the office, but her father sounded terrible, and he was crying. She tried to get him to settle down and explain what was wrong. Finally, he told her that her mother had a stroke and she was in the hospital, and he was there. They haven't told him anything since she arrived there. He was so upset, and he asked Hanna if she could come to Boston. Hanna said she would make arrangements and call him right back.

She hung up the phone and told them at the office what had happened, and they told her to go home and do what she had to. They would manage without her till she got back.

She went home and was so upset not really knowing what to do. She called Grant at his office and told him. He said, "I'll be right over."

She said, "No."

He said," I will be there in a half hour."

In a half hour, she heard a knock at the door, opened it, and there he was. She flew in his arms, and he hugged her and told her things would be okay. He knew her parents lived in Boston, so he told her he was driving her there. He had already made arrangements for someone to take over at work for him, and he made arrangements for Mike at a friend's house. He told her he had a suitcase with clothes in for himself and told her to pack a bag. They would leave as soon as she was ready. Hanna told Grant to call next door for Bobby to feed Gilly while they were gone. He called, and Bobby's mom said they would take care of Gilly, no problem. In fifteen minutes, Hanna was packed, and they went downstairs to the car. Three hours later, they were at the hospital.

Hanna called her father on the phone to find out what floor he was on. He told her third floor. They took the elevator to the third floor waiting room and as they got off the elevator, she saw her father.

He took a second look at both of them when they walked in. He couldn't talk at first to them, and Hanna thought it was bad news, but her father said her mother was okay, and they said she should be okay in a few days. They were keeping her for three days to make sure she would recover with no further problems. Hanna's father kept staring at Grant.

They went home late from the hospital and sat and talked a short time to her father, and then they went to bed. Grant took the guest room, and Hanna was in her old bedroom. Her father laid awake most of the night not worried about Betsy. He was worried about a lifelong secret he kept from his wife, hoping he didn't ever have to tell her about it.

In the morning, as they were eating breakfast, Hanna formally introduced Grant to her father Sam. Told them how they met and about the tragedy of Grant's wife and about his son Mike. Sam told Hanna that her mother had told him some of those details. They finished breakfast, and Sam cleaned up the dishes, but he put Grant's juice glass in a plastic bag, hoping what he was still thinking was not true. Hanna, Grant, and Sam went to the hospital and saw Hanna's mother. She was sitting up in bed and looked good. The doctor told them she had a very mild stroke with no other problems, but he was still going to keep her for two more days to make sure she was fine and to see that the medicine she was going to be taking was agreeing with her. When Grant and Hanna walked in, she saw the likeness Hanna had described to her mother. It was a little shocking. Sam went to Betsy's bedside and gave her a big hug, and tears rolled down his cheek. "I love you so, Betsy," he said.

"Yes, Sam, I know you miss your cook." She chuckled.

They all laughed. Sam said he needed to go downstairs for a moment and get her some magazines to read when they leave. Betsy stated he would bring back all kinds of gifts for her—candy, flowers, and who knows what else.

Sam went straight to the laboratory with the juice glass and Betsy's toothbrush from the bathroom at home. He was hoping nothing came of this fear he had. The tech at the lab would call with the DNA results in about two days. Sam said, "No, I will stop by and pick them up for the results, if that would be okay?"

The tech said that would be fine. Sam gave his name and said he would be back in two days.

He went and picked up a box of candy, flowers, and some magazines and then returned to her room to see them all talking and smiling at each other looking very happy. Sam knew this was hard on Hanna to see her mother ill. They were always close. They sat and talked till after one and then Betsy chased them out to go get some lunch. She said she was tired and needed a nap. They promised to come back after dinner and visit her for a little while.

They all went to lunch, and Grant paid the bill. They went back home and rested for a while and decided ice cream was good enough for dinner, possibly a banana split for all of them. They walked in the hospital to see Betsy sitting in a chair and reading a magazine. She also ate a piece of candy after finishing her dinner. They visited till eight and was chased out by the nurse, telling them she needed her rest. When they were getting ready to leave, Betsy made them promise to go back to Philadelphia the next day. Hanna said she would after she saw her in the morning and talked again to the doctor to know that she was fine before she and Grant would leave.

The next day, Betsy was walking down the hall when they got off the elevator. She looked very good and told them the doctor just left, and she might get discharged tomorrow. She told Grant to take Hanna home and come back in two weeks over the weekend for a visit and bring Michael back with them. She wanted to meet him. Grant promised he would ask him, and he was sure he would like to do that. Grant liked Hanna's parents and knew Michael would like them, too. As much as they both had grown to like Hanna, Betsy knew she would be strong enough to enjoy a visit with all of them again.

So at noon, they left for home after talking to Betsy's doctor. He assured Hanna that her medicine was working fine, and she would have no further problems.

Chapter 9

As they drove home, they were silent for a while. Then they both smiled at each other, and both thought the visit had turned out much better than they thought it would when they started the trip. Hanna thanked Grant for what he did and stated she didn't know how she would ever be able to repay him. He said she already did when she was with his wife at the park when she became ill. Hanna just smiled at him and said, "Now, are we even?"

Grant replied, "We have a long way to go yet, Hanna."

She agreed that they have become very close friends. He dropped her off at her apartment, and she told him again how thankful she was that he went with her and said she would see him soon. He said, "You bet. Good night."

Grant left and picked up Mike, and they went home. Grant told Mike all about Hanna's parents and how nice they were just like Hanna. He told Mike that Hanna's mother was better, that her stroke was very mild. He then told Mike they had an invite from them to come see them for a visit. He told Mike he knew he would enjoy the trip to see them.

The next day was work and school as usual. Hanna went to work and told everyone that her mother was doing fine with a complete recovery.

Sam went to pick up Betsy and stopped at the lab to pick up the results of the test. He was so sure it was nothing he had to be upset about. He took the envelope and stuck it in his pants pocket to look at it later.

He went upstairs to pick up Betsy, and she was ready to leave, wanting to get back home. The doctor came in to say goodbye to both of them and told them that she would be fine, take her medicine and slow down a little. Betsy promised to do both and away they went. Sam was glad to get her home and have things normal again.

Hanna called to see if they were home and to see how her mother felt today. She was surprised when her mother answered the phone and said things were normal again. Not to forget the invite they all had in two weeks.

Hanna promised she wouldn't and told her Grant mentioned it to Michael, and he is excited to come. Her mother sounded happy and said how much she liked Grant. They said goodbye and would keep in touch.

Sam went out to the shed after dinner as usual and remembered the report in his pocket. He opened it up and read the results and fell against the table in the shed. He felt faint. He sat down and put his head in his hands, trying to get his wits about him. He could hardly believe he read the report right, so he looked it over again. He read where it said the results were a "match." This was what he was so afraid of. How would he make the people he loved for so many years make them understand the secret he had kept from them for so many years. Sam sat there and relived the tragedy all over again. It just seemed like it was yesterday that it happened. He thought time would make the terrible tragedy less painful, but it didn't as he remembered it all over again. It was just like it was happening right now.

He remembered his old friend Paul. They spent so many summers together doing things when they were out of school in the summers. Paul had moved to Sam's neighborhood when they were in eighth grade, and they were together every summer from there on till it happened. In tenth grade, Paul told Sam he was dating this neat girl named Betsy. Sam liked sports so he had no time for girls. Betsy and Paul always had time for Sam. They played softball, and Betsy would come and watch the games. That is when Sam got to know Betsy. He was very happy for Paul, but Sam still didn't want a girlfriend. Once in a while, he would go to the movies with a girl he would ask out but never got involved with one. He liked sports too well.

There was a dance after their senior graduation. Paul told Sam that he had asked Betsy to go with him. He told Sam they were getting married right after they all graduated and that Betsy was pregnant. He asked Sam to keep his secret. Sam said, "What are you going to do?"

Paul said his father would give him a job at the store when they got married but didn't want to tell his parents till after they graduated. His father had asked him to come to work for him after he got done with school, and Paul told him he would, so it was already a plan.

The night of the senior ball, Paul asked Sam to go with them. Sam had a date so they double-dated. They all had a great time. Sam thought Betsy looked so pretty that night, and Paul was so in love with her. On the way home, it started to rain and became so foggy it was hard to see. They were hit by a large truck. Paul was killed instantly. Sam and his date were just scratched up and a few bumps. Betsy was thrown from the car and was taken to the hospital. She was in a coma for three weeks. She delivered a premature baby boy weighing three pounds. The baby survived and when Betsy was in the coma, her parents thought it best to adopt the baby out to another couple. They had hopes of Betsy going to college, hoping she would survive the accident. It was a very difficult time for everyone involved.

They made Sam promise to keep their secret from Betsy if she survived to never tell her that the baby lived. They were going to tell Betsy that she lost the baby in the accident. Sam was so upset, but he had no say in the matter, so he made the promise to her parents.

He went every day to the hospital to see Betsy after she came out of the coma. They became very close. Sam missed Paul as much as Betsy did.

When she was told she lost the baby, she went into a depressed state with a lot of counseling before she accepted the loss. Sam was right by her side through the whole time she was healing and was suffering right along with her and trying to heal also. Sam became so sad about her parents' decision and the promise he had made to them. As time went on, he grew to love Betsy and asked her to marry him. She fell deeply in love with him and soon after, he asked her. They were married. Betsy's mother died, and two years later, her father passed away, and Hanna was only one year old. The three of them became a very close family, adoring their daughter. They tried to have more children, but it never happened, so Hanna became their whole life.

Chapter 10

As he sat in his shop, he thought how in the world will he tell his secret to the people he loves so dearly. Who should he tell first? Didn't want to tell Betsy at this time, he decided it would be best to tell Hanna first, and he knew he had to tell Hanna soon. He decided to tell Hanna first and then together they would tell Betsy. Then together they would tell Grant and Michael. He thought that plan would be the best. He knew he had to call Hanna and have her come so he could tell her the whole story. He knew he couldn't wait too long to do this, although he hated to call her again at work, but Betsy was always around in the evening with him, like a little puppy dog since she had the stroke. She was always busy in the daytime cleaning, getting meals, and talking on the phone to her friends, but in the evenings now, it was her time with Sam. Even now, she went to the shop in the evenings to watch him do his woodwork, or she would help him in the garden most of the time. The only time she wasn't with him was when she got a call. He loved her so that he didn't want to tell her she didn't have to do it. So it became a change in their lives.

The next day, Sam knew he had to call Hanna, so he went upstairs after breakfast and shut the door and called Hanna at work. She answered the phone, and it was her father. Hanna became upset, but her father assured her that her mother and he were fine. He just said he had something he was concerned about that he needed her help, to help him fix it, and he needed to do it soon. If she could come home this coming weekend, he would appreciate it. She said, "Dad, are you sure everything is okay?"

Sam said, "Yes, but it is something I should have taken care of a long time ago."

Hanna said she would see them this weekend. After she got off the phone, she decided he probably was overconcerned about willing things to her if something happened to both of them. She relaxed a little about the phone call. She made arrangements for the weekend to go home. She called Grant and told him she thought her father was anxious about talking to her about a will, if something happened to both of them. Grant said he was probably upset about Betsy's sudden illness and was thinking about the future, which was a good thing to take care of soon.

Saturday morning, Hanna caught the commuter and was home in time for lunch. Her mother opened the door and was surprised to see her, but she told her about her dad's phone call, and Betsy said Sam never said a word to her. Sam came in from the garden not knowing Hanna had arrived early. She took a taxi to their home. He kissed her and said she should have called and he would have picked her up. She told him she looked for him but couldn't see him at the station so she just called a cab. Sam wanted to apologize and said he has had a lot on his mind lately. Hanna said, "I know, Dad, so let's go talk."

Sam replied, "After we eat lunch, then you and I can talk while your mother cleans up after lunch, don't need to be bother with us talking."

Betsy said, "Sam, I am fine."

Sam said he knew, but he and Hanna could work it out together.

So they had a nice lunch together and small talk. After lunch, Sam stated he wanted Hanna to help him first in the garden with something, then they would be in to finish talking. So away they went to do what Sam needed done.

As they walked to the garden, Hanna noticed how upset her father had become. "Dad, what are you so upset about?"

Her dad looked at her and said, "I need to tell you something that will affect the whole family, and I don't know where to start and how to tell all of you."

Hanna asked, "Dad, are you sure it will affect all of us?"

Her father stated, "Yes, Hanna."

"Well, Dad, you better start to tell me about it."

Hanna's father sat down on a stool in the shed and motioned her to sit in the other one. Hanna sat down, and Sam started to tell Hanna the story and the secret he kept all these years.

He started by telling her about the friendship he had with Paul and Betsy. Sam then told her about the night of their graduation and the terrible weather before the accident happened. He told her next about the details about how they all were hurt. Then he told her about the coma Betsy was in for three weeks and the birth of her baby boy and the promise her parents made him promise to keep from her. Sam lowered his head, and tears started to form in his eyes. Then he looked up at his daughter and was shocked to see the look on her face. Her face was as white as snow. He couldn't stop yet. He had to finish everything he knew. He then told her how he fell in love with Betsy and how he has kept the secret from her because he thought it best after they had Hanna. They were all so happy, and he felt he didn't want to change that closeness with Betsy. Her parents hadn't died till after Betsy had Hanna, so right or wrong, he kept the secret he had promised Betsy's parents.

When he saw Grant, he was shocked about the likeness and thought about the adoption and his age, but thought it couldn't possibly be Betsy's baby. He became alarmed about a relationship that might happen between Hanna and Grant and had to prove there was nothing to what he was alarmed about. He decided to prove it was nothing to worry about so he decided to do a DNA testing to rule it out. He did the test when Betsy was in the hospital and Grant came to visit, about the juice glass and the toothbrush of Betsy.

In short, he told Hanna it was a "match." He said he became so upset he need to tell her right away, and he hoped she understood and still loved him for possibly a mistake he made. Hanna sat in shock at the whole story. Her father got up and walked over to her, gave her a kiss on the cheek, and started to cry. Hanna got up and hugged her father. She didn't know what to say. She was totally taken back by all the information she now was told about her family and now about Grant. She knew her father was telling her the truth. Now, what were they going to do about all this? She looked into her father's face and said, "What do we do now, Dad?"

Sam was worried about telling Hanna's mother so soon after her stroke. Hanna said that they maybe should tell Grant now. She wanted her father to tell him the part about the accident first and then about the DNA testing.

They decided to tell Betsy it was about the will. That is why he wanted to talk to Hanna this weekend and that they were going to have Grant next weekend help them with some of the legal items they have discussed today. They planned to ask Betsy to do something with Mike while they told Grant next weekend. They were happy with their plan so far with telling Grant the truth. Both were still heartbroken of the secret her father had to live with for such a long time. He never felt bad about it till he found out with the testing and was forced to face the whole incident and telling everyone the truth and the secret promise he made. In his mind, he thought he would die with the secret, but it was not to be, so he was facing it with all the strength he had to do the right thing now. They told Betsy what they were doing about making a will, and they were going to have Grant help them with some legal issues when he came up next weekend to visit. She agreed it was a great idea. They had coffee and cookies Betsy had gotten ready while they were outside talking.

Hanna and Sam didn't seem very hungry, and Betsy was surprised because they usually fought over her fresh baked cookies. They said they must have talked and worked too hard. They went to town for a light dinner and came back and played some cards. They went to bed, but Hanna didn't sleep very well; neither did her father. Both looked tired when they all said goodbye. Hanna said she would see them next weekend with Grant and Mike.

Grant called and asked if everything went well, and Hanna said that her dad wanted to see him about the will he wanted to have done when they all came up next weekend. Grant said he would be glad to help in any way he could. Grant said Mike was so excited about the visit and then they said good night and hung up.

Hanna hardly slept at all that whole week. She went out with Grant and Michael to a movie but said she was so tired and after the movie went straight home. Saturday came and they met at the commuter station. Got on and they had breakfast in the dining car. They sat and talked a while, mostly Mike did the chatting. He was so excited to make the trip. After a while, they returned to their seat on the train.

Grant felt like Hanna's heart wasn't in it for this visit and wondered if they should have come for the visit, but she said she was just so tired. It was such a busy week and visiting her parents last weekend put her off schedule. She loved visiting her parents, but she has always paced herself on not overdoing it. He said that maybe they should have come next week, but she said, "No, her father wanted to settle this matter as soon as possible." Something in her voice made Grant feel funny.

Mike was so excited to visit with her parents, and Grant promised to show him around Boston. There was no turning back now. The train stopped, and Hanna's father was there to pick them up. They got to the house in no time, and Betsy was at the door to welcome them. Everyone had a great lunch that Betsy had made. Grant said the trip was worth it for her cooking. Mike seconded the motion, and Betsy said, "Just wait till you eat dinner."

In the meantime, Hanna said, "Dad and I and Grant should get our business done."

Her father picked up on it and said, "Oh, right."

Betsy said, "Mike and I will go out back and feed the birds and take a walk while you guys do business."

Mike agreed.

The three of them went to Sam's den. Sam told Grant and Hanna to have a seat, and then Hanna told Grant that the will was not the reason they needed to talk. It was about something else they needed to tell him. So Sam proceeded to tell Grant the story about the accident when they were in high school. Grant wondered why he needed to tell him this. Sam knew he was confused and Sam stated, "Grant, just bear with me. You will soon understand."

He talked about his friend Paul and Betsy and their plans after high school. Then he picked up on the details again about the accident. He told them about the coma Betsy was in after the accident and then told them about the birth of a baby boy and what her parents made him promise about the adoption. He fell in love with Betsy during her recovery, and they were married. He stated how he felt till Hanna was born, and then he grew to think it was okay to keep the secret. Betsy's parents died about a year after Hanna was born. First her mother and then her father, so the promise became less important to them. They were very happy. He also told Grant about Betsy's depression after her parents told her that her baby died when she was in the coma.

Sam said that when he saw Grant at the hospital, he was shocked at the resemblance to Hanna. That was when he knew he had to do a DNA testing. He looked at Grant as he listened quietly to all Sam was telling him. "Betsy is your maternal mother. The test came back a match." He told him about the juice glass and Betsy's toothbrush. Grant stood up and walked to the den window. He saw Mike and Betsy feeding the birds and smiled. He turned around and said, "I knew I loved you, Hanna, when you kissed me on my cheek. Now I know I love your family when I looked out the window and see my mother with my son feeding the birds."

They all started to hug each other and cried.

Now, the question is how do we tell Betsy? Sam said he didn't want to tell her this weekend. He wanted to wait till he had a chance to talk to her doctor and find out the best way to tell her this secret.

He wanted to talk to her doctor first. It seemed too risky to tell her before they asked her doctor. They agreed and thought they would wait till Sam saw her doctor and see how he thought they should handle this and when.

They went outside. All were smiling as they saw Mike and Betsy feeding the squirrels now and laughing themselves.

They all went in the house to have dinner. Betsy had fixed meatloaf. Grant smiled and said he has had it before and Hanna said, "Mom's is much better."

Grant said he thought it was true. Hanna laughed and slapped him on his arm. Then they decided to play a game and then went to bed early. All were very tired. Got up the next day to leave and Mike said he wished they lived closer; that Sam had promised when they came back for another visit, he would show Mike how to make a birdhouse. Grant looked at Hanna and smiled. He knew how much she loved both of them, and now he was growing to know why. He realized how lucky they were now. She now knew she had a great brother and an adorable nephew. Soon she would be able to tell everyone and claim her additional family publicly.

They got to the station and took their seats; read most of the way home. When they got to Philadelphia, they kissed each other on the cheek and said goodbye. She smiled at the boys and got in her car and waved goodbye.

Chapter 11

Sam sat in the living room looking at Betsy. She seemed so happy. He said, "Did you have a good time with Mike and Grant?"

She looked at him and said, "If Hanna ever has a little boy someday, I would want him to be just like Mike. He is such a sweet kid."

Sam looked at her and thought if she only knew. He just said, "Me, too." He was still wondering how she was going to react when he told her about the secret he had kept from her all these years. He was hoping the doctor would let him tell her soon all about it. He wanted to unload this burden he carried for so long.

The next day, Hanna called her father and was worried about him doing this on his own. She promised to take a day off and meet him when he talked to the doctor. Sam said he would call her and tell her when to be here. She told Grant about coming, and he said he would come with her when Sam called. She told her father Grant was driving her up to come also. After all, it was his mother now, too, they were talking about.

They came up for the appointment, and Sam was sitting in the doctor's office when they got there. Sam started to tell the doctor the whole story, and the doctor said it would be fine to tell her, but he wanted them all to meet at the hospital in his office to tell her where they could monitor her afterwards for an hour or two. They agreed and set up the appointment.

She went for the appointment not knowing what was in store for her, thinking it was a follow-up to her hospital stay. When she got there and saw Grant and Hanna, she became alarmed, but the doctor assured her she would be happy they were there. She sat down, and Sam started to tell her about the accident that happened so long ago. Betsy couldn't figure out how she would be happy about this. When Sam got to the part about the promise he had to make to her parents, she started to cry. When he told her what they made him promise, when he told her she gave birth to a little baby boy and that they decided it best to tell Betsy at that time the baby died, that the baby was adopted out to unknown parents, all Betsy could do was cry. She looked at Grant, and he smiled. Sam didn't need to tell her about the DNA testing he had done. She knew Grant was her son. Betsy got up and Grant got up, and she hugged him and kissed him and cried with happiness of knowing the truth. She went over to Sam sitting in his chair and tears streaming down his cheeks. She kissed him, still crying for what her parents had done to him for all these years.

Hanna sat smiling with tears rolling down her cheeks, knowing the burden was gone, and she could enjoy and love her family, thinking how blessed that they were at last. She was smiling at all of them as she looked at them taking it all in, even the doctor with happiness. She now had a brother and a nephew.

She couldn't wait now to tell Mike. They were all pretty sure he would be delighted. The doctor took Betsy's vitals and said she was fine and that they should all go celebrate and have a party. Betsy and Sam agreed. They went to the donut shop and had coffee and donuts. Hanna and Grant had to get back to Philadelphia for Mike. The whole way home, Grant and Hanna thought of how they would tell Mike.

They decided they would take Mike up to Sam and Betsy's for his ninth birthday in two weeks and on the cake, they would put Grandma and Pappy to Mike. Hanna called her parents and told them the idea, and they were all for it. So Grant told Mike they were going back to Boston with Hanna and celebrate his birthday with her parents. Mike was all excited about it.

They got there, and the house was all decorated inside with balloons and crepe paper. Presents were everywhere. Mike was so happy. They ate lunch, and then Betsy said they invited some friends to come over from the neighborhood. Mike asked, "Will they bring presents, too?"

Grant growled him out, but Betsy said, "I bet they will."

Mike could hardly wait for the party to start. He was sitting in the room watching a movie when Betsy carried the cake in, and the cake said, "Happy Birthday, Mike, from Grandma and Pappy!" Mike looked at it and smiled but looked puzzled. Grant whispered in his ear, "I will tell you later." Mike was so excited with all the presents and the people and the food that it slipped his mind. They had a great time laughing and talking and playing with the toys and games. There were kids his age who were neighbors, which made Mike really happy and enjoy his party more. Betsy and Sam were so happy for him. After all, he has been through at his age and still remain such a great boy.

After the party, Grant and Hanna took Mike up to his room and sat with him and told Mike the highlights of the story about his father and Betsy, and the promise Sam had to keep from her. Mike was so tired; he remembered that Betsy was his father's real mother and that made her his grandmother, and Sam was his pappy. He was so happy when he fell asleep. When he got awake the next day, he asked his dad if it was a dream. His father told him, "No. They are your grandparents," and he smiled and went in the kitchen and hugged both of them and called them Grandma and Pappy. They got tears in their eyes and asked him what he wanted for breakfast, and he said, "Whatever you are having."

Grant and Hanna were cleaning up the backyard after the party. They came in to see them eating and smiling at each other, enjoying their breakfast together. Sam said to Mike, "We better hurry and eat. We have a birdhouse to build."

At that thought, Mike started to finish his breakfast in a hurry and away they went. Betsy, Hanna, and Grant sat there with their second cup of coffee. After a while, Grant got up and said, "I think I will go see what Sam and Mike are up to." He saw them with a half-finished birdhouse. Grant pitched in, and it was ready to paint. Grant said, "Let's take it home and paint it, and we can hang it out at our house, and maybe, Grandma and Pap will come see it at our house soon."

So they agreed to do that. "They need to come and see where we live now," Grant stated, and Mike joined him.

Chapter 12

It was going to be the Fourth of July, and Grant thought it would be great to have everyone at his house for a backyard picnic, so he called Hanna. "Hey, sis, I want Mom and Dad to come on the Fourth of July for a picnic in the backyard. What do you think of that? Mike and I want them to spend some time here with us to get to know us more." Hanna thought that would be good for all of them. It will be great for all of us to spend some happy time together. Grant called his parents, and they said they would be happy to spend the Fourth with all of them.

Hanna, Grant, and Mike had a great time preparing for the get-together. Grant decided to call Ted—coworker and best friend—to come to the picnic. Ted said he would be glad to meet his new family. Mike showed his pap the birdhouse he painted. Sam said it looked great, but they needed another one in the tree out front. "Next time you come up," Sam stated, "I have a new pattern for a different style one, and we would build it."

Mike was happy and said maybe next weekend, and Sam laughed. The food was great, and they all had fun in the backyard. They watched some fireworks someone had and watched a beautiful sunset from the yard. Grant was so happy to share this with his new family and best buddy. Hanna and family met

Ted, Grant's best friend. When everyone left to go to Hanna's apartment, Ted asked Grant if he would care if he asked Hanna to go to dinner with him.

Grant said, "Go for it."

Ted laughed and said, "Okay, buddy."

Ted called Hanna the next week, and they went to dinner. They had a great time, and they saw each other a lot in the next few months. By Christmas, Hanna and Ted—at a party the family was having—made an announcement that they were getting married.

Grant said, "I said you could take her out for dinner."

They all laughed and were delighted for them both. They all had Christmas at Grant's house. What a long way they had all come to find each other and happiness. This Christmas season, they all knew how lucky they had become through all their sorrow.

As they sat at the Christmas tree, after everyone went to bed, Hanna could see Grant had something on his mind. She thought it was Ella. Grant said, "No, I was just thinking of my real father who never had a chance to know any of this."

Hanna said, "I am sure Dad has a year-book with your father's picture in it, so you could see him. I am also sure Dad and Mom will tell you about him, too, so you will know a little bit about him."

Grant looked at his sister and said, "I love you, sis. You are the best, and now you are marrying my best friend. You have filled Mike and my life with so much happiness since I have met you. It just doesn't get any better!"

Hanna got up, leaned over him, and said, "May I kiss you, Big Brother?"

They both laughed.